D1505029

The Very NOISY Night

by Diana Hendry
illustrated by Jane Chapman

PUFFIN BOOKS

It was the middle of the night, and Big Mouse was fast asleep in his big bed. Little Mouse was wide awake in his little bed.

"Big Mouse! Big Mouse!" called Little Mouse. "I can hear something rushing around the house, huffing and puffing."

Big Mouse opened one eye and lifted
one ear. "It's only the wind," he said.

"Can I come into your bed?"
asked Little Mouse.

"No," said Big Mouse. "There isn't room." And
he turned over and went back to sleep.

Little Mouse lay listening
to the wind. Then suddenly,
between a huff and a puff,
came a . . .

TAP

TAP

TAP

TAP

Little Mouse climbed out of bed, opened
the front door—just a crack—and peeped out.

WHOOOSH!

went the wind, but there was no one outside.

"Big Mouse! Big Mouse!" called Little Mouse. "I can hear someone tapping. I think there's a burglar on the roof."

Big Mouse got out of
bed and opened the bedroom
curtains. "Look," he said. "It's only
a branch tapping on the window.
Go back to sleep."

"Can I come into your bed?"
asked Little Mouse.

"No," said Big Mouse. "You
wriggle."

Little Mouse lay in his own bed and listened to the wind huffing and puffing and the branch tap-tapping—and someone calling,

"HOO-HOO!

HOO-HOO!"

Little Mouse climbed out of bed again. This time he looked under it. Then he looked in the wardrobe, and feeling very frightened, he yelled, "Big Mouse! Big Mouse! I think there's a ghost in the room, and it's looking for someone. It keeps calling, 'Who-who, who-who!'"

Big Mouse sighed, sat up, and listened. "It's only an owl," he said. "It stays up all night, like you."

"Can I come into your bed?" asked Little Mouse.

"No," said Big Mouse. "Your paws are always cold." Big Mouse pulled the blanket over his head and went back to sleep, and Little Mouse got back into his own bed.

Little Mouse sat up and listened to the wind huffing and puffing, and the branch tap-tapping, and the owl hooting. But *shhh!* What was that?

"Big Mouse! Big Mouse!" he called.
I think it's raining inside." And Little Mouse jumped
out of bed and fetched his red umbrella.

DRIP
DRIP
DRIP
DRIP

Big Mouse got out of bed, too. He opened the front door to see if it was raining at all. Then Big Mouse went into the kitchen and turned off the dripping faucet. He gently pried the umbrella out of Little Mouse's paws and put it away.

"Can I come into your bed?"
asked Little Mouse.

"No, you're nice and snug in your own bed," said
Big Mouse, taking him back to the bedroom.

Little Mouse lay and listened
to the wind huffing and puffing,
the branch tap-tapping, and the
owl hooting. And just as he was
beginning to feel very sleepy
indeed, he heard . . .

"WHEEE,
WHEEE,
WHEEEEE!"

"Big Mouse! Big Mouse!"
he called. "You're snoring."

Wearily, Big Mouse got up. He put his earmuffs on Little Mouse's ears. He put a paper clip on his own nose, and he went back to bed.

Little Mouse lay and listened to—nothing!
It was very, very, very quiet. He couldn't hear
the wind huffing or the branch tapping or the owl
hooting or Big Mouse snoring. It was so quiet that
Little Mouse felt he was all alone in the world.

He took off the earmuffs. He got out of bed
and pulled the paper clip off Big Mouse's nose.
"Big Mouse! Big Mouse!" he cried. "I'm lonely!"

Big Mouse flung back his blanket. "Better come into my bed," he said. So Little Mouse hopped in, and his paws were cold . . .

and he needed just a little wriggle before he fell fast asleep.

Big Mouse lay and listened to the wind huffing and puffing and the branch tap-tapping and the owl hooting and Little Mouse snuffling, and very soon he heard the birds waking up. But neither of them heard the alarm clock . . .

BECAUSE THEY WERE
BOTH FAST ASLEEP!

For Emelia
—D.H.

For Anthony, Jane, Mark,
Katy, and Alice, with love
—J.C.

PUFFIN BOOKS
Published by the Penguin Group
Penguin Putnam Books for Young Readers, 345 Hudson Street, New York, New York 10014, U.S.A.
Penguin Books Ltd, 27 Wrights Lane, London W8 5TZ, England
Penguin Books Australia Ltd, Ringwood, Victoria, Australia
Penguin Books Canada Ltd, 10 Alcorn Avenue, Toronto, Ontario, Canada M4V 3B2
Penguin Books (N.Z.) Ltd, 182-190 Wairau Road, Auckland 10, New Zealand
Penguin Books Ltd, Registered Offices: Harmondsworth, Middlesex, England

First published in the United States of America by Dutton Children's Books,
a division of Penguin Putnam Books for Young Readers, 1999
Originally published in the United Kingdom by Little Tiger Press, London, 1999
Published by Puffin Books, a division of Penguin Putnam Books for Young Readers, 2001

10 9 8 7 6 5

Text copyright © Diana Hendry, 1999.   Illustrations copyright © Jane Chapman, 1999.   All rights reserved.

CIP Data is available.

Puffin Books ISBN 0-14-230012-8

Manufactured in China